Unfinished Love

Seven mini stories that'll speak to the love in your heart

Deepti Kolte

HOLISTIC Publishing

Published by "The Great Indian Book Tour"
Imprint : Holistic Publishing
www.tgibt.com
106/91, Ashok marg, Vijay path
Mansarover, Jaipur, Rajasthan-302020
Phone : +91-72400-68114
email : prashant@tgibt.com

Title : Unfinished Love: Seven mini stories that'll speak to the love in your heart
Author : Deepti Kolte

First published in 2025
First Edition 2025
Printed in India
Printer : Repro Printers
ISBN : 978-93-49571-59-4
Price : 150

To the love in your Heart

Contents

Preface

When you experience love in its truest and purest form, your unexplored and subdued parts find a home. You wake up every day, a slightly altered person with a feeling of a certain nonspecific contemplation — of moments you would relive over and again, in despair and in joy.

You behold your inner world with the eyes of a sunflower, in night and in day.

As such *the love* found and lived not in the years but in those moments — continues.

The book is a collection of mini fictional stories of such unfinished love. I couldn't help but infuse them with a little poetry.

I have written it from the mind of a woman as that came naturally to me in the flow of writing the stories. Regardless, I hope it will speak to the love in your heart.

♥♥♥

Broken, it cried empty,
Suspended in a vortex of pain,
Curled up smaller and smaller,
To be lost in dark somewhere.
Heart lies wrapped crestfallen.
Love does that.

Its cracks mended with gold,
eeded with the longing for self,
It unspools radiating vaster,
With unaware of joys.
Heart is unwrapped buoyant.
Love does that.

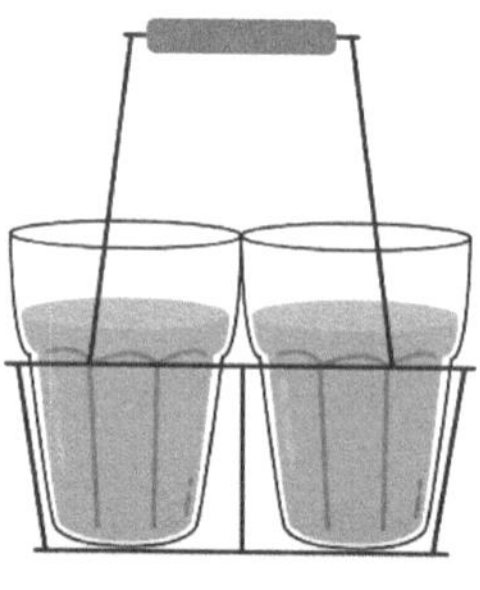

Impromptu

Ambling along the sidewalk,

Hopping over an idle stone,

Pulling at a branch dangling over a fence,

Tossing a ball kicked at them by a gaggle of kids,

Curious musings about the passersby,

Her longing looks at the flower shop,

His shaking a tree to let the flowers fall in her cupped hands,

Letting the turns of the lanes lead them, although getting startled by sudden intercepting stray beings they were both scared of.

This — not a bucket list but the trinkets of their impromptu day of sorts.

They rested on the steps of a corner chai shop, no better nectar than a warm cup of tea for these improvised, tired butterflies. They had forgotten their phones at home, the perk of an impromptu walk. But the small change money in their denim pockets got them a few glasses of the cutting chai. Trivia on evolution, the size of the universe, the why and how of things, just some of the random topics their brains swirled while enjoying their chai.

When it felt like it was time to head back, but the day was still alive for more randomness, they saw a not so busy chaat stall in their lane. By then they were left with no money, having splurged it on their little parTEA! But the craving for nippattu masala chaat was overpowering. He asked and she said yes. And while she wiped her dripping eyes triggered by the pepper-spicy, grated carrot topped chaat, he memorized the chaat wallahs mobile number. Fascinating, that the chaat wallah easily trusted him with doing that. And so, he sent him the money when they got their mobile phones.

She wasn't sure if she'll get the same moments and the same day twice. But a little spontaneity as part of the daily choices is how she would chance upon small joys and the love that rides with it, everyday. She felt sure about it that day.

Once she played with the football in a saree because she was wearing a saree and he had the football in his hands, so why not!

When there is no quest for an unknown missing piece in the next moment, when you are full with the enoughness in the present, it creates space for love to breathe, to thrive. Love has more than thrived for her and within her.

One day she followed a butterfly and its little trail led her to a bunch of yellow, wild flowers. She had never noticed them before, although they are a common sight. How alive she felt that day! As if she had an epiphany of the wings she possessed, those that were glued by the planned and the routines.

On a new year's, he wished her to *Be Boundless.*

Perhaps he left because he wanted to be boundless himself.

Whenever she looks up at the boundless blue that is bright with the soft, sunny, muted undertone, she wants to remind him of the yellow.

Being boundless didn't have to be all blue.

But instead of muting the pain within her, she lets the old thoughts recycle into the new moments and lets the randomness, fuel their churning, like a fodder for the soul, haloed by the spontaneity.

♥♥♥

Moonfeels

"The most beautiful fixture in the night sky", they both looked up wonder-smitten.

Vikram lander of the Chandrayaan-2 mission, must be there somewhere on the moon's surface. It had just been a few days since the lunar crashing. "Every time I look at the moon these days, I feel a sense of belonging towards it knowing that the lander from our country is there." And he smiled and nodded, a moment of syzygy; the moon, him and her!

There was such an exciting, affectionate intimacy in this moment. When your thoughts feel so unique to you, you don't imagine anyone else could be thinking the same, because they might seem unusual or maybe a bit metaphysical. But then, when you find someone who not just relates, but feels them, it makes you think love is real!

Over the rooftop — under the moon — counting the stars — she felt the twinkling of the shared stardust in her heart.

Gaping at the hugeness of the cosmos together, she was awe-love-struck.

"Let's count the stars" she said casually. The excitement of watching the sky together had gotten her in a playful mood.

He said, "yes" just as playfully.

As if teasing with their blink and miss game, the stars also joined in their play.

Watching the moon break into the undulating clouds, parts of her heart were constellating, mapping them out on the night sky with stories that have never been heard, with stories stowed away in the compartments of her heart. And the rest of it was filled with a quiet conversation between two moon-ecstatic beings observing the wonders of the starry sky.

She shared with him her favourite part from her trip to a hill station; the bejewelled night sky over the hills with stars in every line of sight. It felt like being ambushed by happiness. A memory so vivid, yet this was the first time she was talking about it.

But tonight, watching the relatively sparsely stellar sky with him was similar to watching a celestial event to her.

A moment when she experienced what 'love is' or rather 'could be'.

When they could count no more, the talk in their shared silence was really about listening to each other's admiration for the ineffable expanse and infinity they were both enchanted with, perhaps in the same measure. Mingling the moonlight and the shafts of starlight in their moments, they lived a lifetime of love in those.

One day he wanted it to be the last time they met and mentioned something about it being a good riddance for her.

She has crossed paths with the moon so many times without realizing how much it'll matter in her future season of being. She looks up now not by the force of habit but knowing he would be looking at it and adoring just the same.

The moon prints are not waning and the waxing crescent of the moon mends the ache. And so, she goes on — *the sum of the moonbeams she soaked in with him.*

Sometimes the vast infinitum,

Empty filled with vacuum,

To the eyes under,

Looks dark and darker.

But on the other side,

The orb of the night,

Remains. Shines.

And thus, every time,

The broken heals,

With, the Moonfeels.

♥♥♥

Bol

Growing up as a child, tabla was her favourite musical instrument. The interest paled with life taking its course, until she met him.

After they had met more than once, she thought they could do more than coffee dates.

He said yes to the first thing she suggested, a musical concert. The timing of the concert was an exhilarating synchronicity. And she was trying to contain it in the hush between her heartbeats. Attending such a musical performance was going to be a first of its kind for her.

Both of them didn't talk much while in commute to the concert.

They were busy absorbing the din of the traffic on the potholed roads while processing the flutter in their hearts, the kind that happens in the early days of dating. All autorickshaws have a dangerously protruding screw bolt on the insides. A concerned her noticed it only that day because he was sitting too close to it. That was pretty much the talking they did.

Till date the screw bolt in any auto takes her back to that moment.

Since they reached just in time, only the last rows were left for their taking. Afterall it was Ustad Zakir Hussain's concert.

The performance had their full attention for the entire duration, at least 80% of hers. Apart from how divine the music was, she wanted to be able to talk keenly to him about the entirety of it later on. The rest 20% of the time she was observing him with an occasional glance to see if he was enjoying it, and if they were enjoying the same things, the same way.

The trifecta of them together and the magical bol* of Ustad Zakir Hussain's tabla etched the evening in her heart forever. To her, it felt like a soothing hug from the past.

It is amazing, how two unrelated people can enjoy and love the same music, isn't it? It was like sharing love notes over a symphony they didn't imagine could tune them together.

She always had the affinity to classical music. And it needed just one love spark to ignite this latent love.

She hums to herself,

On clear winter mornings,

On a sinking day,

In soul stirring chaos,

On walks of joy,

If only for a moment —

Everything is radiant,

With the music you gave me.

Like a chorus it keeps me company.

I start at the beginning,

Of the songs I discovered with you.

They were strangely always a part of me.

But when a song ends abruptly, the heart sinks under the weight of the quiet. She did cry an ocean when it did and drowned in it for a while. But now she holds on to the intermezzos and the bol of the tabla.

The thing about music is —

It lights you up.

The thing about love is —

It shows you the light.

The heart holds in a lot more than it speaks. So sometimes she sings in that light.

Heart tapping of a broken heart, of the heart in love — is it different? Maybe. Hers is filled with the love notes over a symphony.

***Bol** - *Syllable or note played on the tabla.*

♥♥♥

A Green Hug

She thought of him yet again.

The delicate five petalled whorls, their gilded smiles, the tuft of frangipani flowers, rivetted her yet again.

"Just look at its height, imagine how old this plant must be." His voice cracked affectionately. The plumeria tree in his backyard garden swayed gently.

There was a sapling he had planted just outside his gate that had turned almost leafless a week ago. But it was starting to bear green shoots now. It was heartening for her to see the tiny hope in his eyes when he had caressed the little new leaves.

There are moments in life that graze your suppressed parts and infuse it with life again —

That day a half of his dinner table was preciously covered with the spread of Rajnigandha flower bulbs. He didn't want even a single one of them to be lost.

Not sure if they ever bloomed.

She didn't think twice before soiling her hands to plant them along with him as she normally would have. Sometimes she used to do gardening with her grandfather in her childhood. It was just a simple memory that got triggered in that moment and she shared it with him.

Those were the moments for her.

She loved trees and flowers. But after she met him, there was more. She gave more and deliberate attention to them, spent more and intentional time with nature.

She was noticing things she hadn't before and in a way that was new and refreshing to her; as rare as a sparrow on a bamboo tree. A plumeria tree adorned in its sweet, mildly scented flowers takes her back to his moment of affection with his tree, every time.

She notices the trees are tall and the sunlight is softly forking through their branches.

She sees through them all.

Just the way they did on their walks.

He could meditate on a tree. And become one with it — calmly rooted, strong and welcoming to all kinds of beings. Earthly.

She reflects as she saunters through,

The meanderings,

Through by-the-way blocks,

And distant parks and trails.

The unblushing tall trees,

Their shy crowns,

The unkempt grass green,

Crewelling the earthly brown,

With the needle like bristles of the awn.

The peace in the shadows,

The earthy cool touch of the soil under,

A tree.

I wonder,

Why I love my walks.

And then sometimes she finds a big sprawling banyan tree, a tabebuia tree awash in pink blossoms or a copperpod in her treasured walks. Alternating between seasons she sits in front of them, observes, meditates.

In the boughs of the branches laden with leaves in their oval, linear, elliptical shapes patterned, curled, swaying linear — in the shade of a tree, the foliage carpeting beneath — the flowers in the pots in the balconies — the fluffy cottonlike fibre stuffed in a fruit of an unknown, unnamed tree that they discovered in one of their leisure walks in a small side park lined with tall trees in a late evening — the white soft fibre floating out of the fruits as if snowflakes had miracled in the park that night — the tree they hugged.

In them an unfinished story lingers. That's where the love is stored.

♥♥♥

Just Be

"Just Be!" The words that would open a portal to self like never before.

On a cozy December evening, a girl and a boy met in a city. They started getting to know each other. There were times when messages would dry up. And there were times when replies would get delayed in between work. She used to get very apologetic about that. The early days are tender, aren't they?

"I am ok with the silence", he said to her one day and that has stuck with her since then.

They started spending time with each other doing things sometimes; doing nothing a lot of times. Sitting quietly with each other sometimes; doing their own things while being with each other a lot of times.

He watched by the sides while she cooked.

They read their own in different corners.

She took a short walk and let him finish his reading.

He dealt with his mundane while she finished her mundane.

Atop a peak, they watched the clouds float and the aerobics of the dragonflies. They observed and felt the rockiness of the hills. They marvelled at the temple carvings. They softened in the sun smiling through the spaces in the shy crowns of the trees.

Somewhere they watched the sun setting behind the clouds, until it kept getting prettier, and waited out to see if it travels below the clouds. When they spotted a near deer shape in the clouds at the back drop of the gorgeous sunset colours while absorbing the distant sounds in the atmosphere, they were just two people living in the moment.

With each other, in quietude, watching the light fall of the leaves under the sombre winter sun, eons could have passed with them just being and not rushing towards what's next. Just being — a feeling so vascular and transient, of letting love flow, not bound by the expectations but by letting it germinate in the stillness of the crisp air — in nothingness.

Such moments tugged at a part of her which only knew of being on the go, of constantly trying, of making things happen, of working it out, of living in a sense of urgency.

Eventually their paths diverged.

Sitting on the half-occupied park bench and staring at the inaccessible inner garden circle, layered with late winter foliage and twigs covered in bright orange, fallen blooms ready to become one with the earth or get whisked away by the occasional breeze — she felt the moist of a tear.

In that moment of letting go, heartbroken, she sat with herself looking up at the light in the trees. "Just Be", she was as if breathing in his words.

With the *just being* as if she felt the connection she had made with herself.

Love didn't seep away from the broken heart. It flows in her smile that does not just stay on her lips, but grows, takes over the eyes and makes the face go crimson with joy, every time she watches a bird soar high in the blue sky, every time she notices a balancing dragonfly and redraws the boundaries of *self* in her quiet moments of being.

♥♥♥

A Rain and a Dance

The evening was lambent in an anxious blush.

The ash grey clouds had scattered a tint of coral pink. Under its patronage she was enroute to meet him for the first time.

He had selected a famous Darshini for them to meet. *Simple is good, takes off the pressure,* her nerves eased at the thought.

He was late and she used the time to grab a stand in the crowded space. When he saw her from a distance, she was smiling and not upset, and that had calmed his nerves.

Quick bites of khara bhath, kesari bhath and filter coffee didn't take long to finish. It turned into her treat. And the only part he minded was that she got off for a cheap one. Since there was no place to sit and have conversation, they eased into a walk.

Seemed like a good start although less typical, she thought.

The breeze was blushing in the satin orange, splitting through the now heavier clouds. In the moisture laden breeze, their hands brushed against each other for a split second.

Shortly after as they reached his place with a flourishing garden, it started drizzling, the kind that makes her want to spread her arms and feel it's warming cold drops caress her face.

Don't know how, but she did just that!

His mirroring of her graceful aplomb, unseated her heart enough to waltz into his arms and swirl in the rhythm of the falling rain; the tilting, pitching heart was floored unflappable.

"My moment of living a long-coveted moment of finding someone who loves to dance", he whispered to her. The rain had arrived as if to say the heavens were in agreement, setting this up all along.

It was surreal. The moment when she felt like she had it all. The moment when it felt like falling in love. The moment when a side of hers was unlayered which she had lived and pictured only in her imagination.

A moment of osmosis when she rediscovered rain —

Rain is joy with wings of love,

That soars like the rose bearing dove,

Rain is an embrace that frees the heart,

That fills itself with the melodies of Mozart.

The rain droplets aren't meant to stay. They are meant to flow. She vainly attempted to collect the dancing rain in her palms as he continued to watch her endearingly. She made it a part of their dance as they moved to the rhythm of the drizzle. That evening the rain touched her in a way it hadn't before, with love.

The rain stopped after sometime, so did their little dance, so did the beautiful evening. How she wished it to be only an intermission; she continues to hold that wish.

They say thoughts become things. And then she wonders how it suddenly starts to rain. Sometimes she witnesses it from behind the window rails, sometimes watches it sipping coffee in a Darshini and sometimes walks right through getting all drenched.

And as such, July rainy evenings arrive and fade, but every time her heart gets soaked with its love.

♥♥♥

The Peacock Colours

It is fascinating and equally remarkable how unrelated moments can inspire each other, effected by love.

It was one of those nice weekend afternoons when the evening seemed to be pushing for its early, *peachy*, breezy arrival and a chance of light rain. In the cosiness of the indoors, they chose to draw together; the view from the window, their muse.

A big green tree brimming with little leaves and a little swing in the home garden and both of them perched on it; the sketch was done soon. By night time they had painted all the many leaves and branches in their sketch.

Exhausted, they left their we-perched-on-swing part uncoloured. It is still unfinished. Life must have happened.

All of this painting and sketching had stirred a treasured memory for him —

Once on one of his solo odysseys, he was looking for shade and spotted a group of street children playing under a lone tree. Watching their carefree antics up close, made him want to get something for them. So, he got colours and drawing kits from a small stationary shop. He showed her a few pictures of their ecstatic smiles.

In that moment, she felt so sweetly proud of him, like in love.

Fancy helium balloons in *pinks* and *blues* with cartoon characters and superheroes printed on them stringed to a balloon cart manned by three kids — a week earlier she saw a colour pop in front of the temple. The kids looked engrossed in their little world of chatter until a car's window rolled down. A balloon with frozen princess pictures — sold.

They kept pushing their little cart around while also doing what children usually do; just be and have fun with whatever there is. She watched them from a distance, thinking to herself that maybe she should do something for them.

Today evening when she saw those kids again, she knew what she could do. She rushed to the closest gift shop and got few sets of crayons and colouring books, gift wrapped in purple shiny paper. By the time she was done, they had moved far ahead and she could only spot their balloons tossing in the breeze. Three young girls accompanied by their aunt; she hurried to catch up with them. When she gave them the gift-wrapped drawing kits, they looked amused and smiled coyly at each other.

Perhaps not sure what else to do, they started to leave.

But then she insisted they open their gifts. While the aunt stood by the cart, all of them sat on the steps of the nearby shop. She asked the girls if they went to school, where they lived, if they liked to draw and so on as they were unwrapping. But they were too engrossed in the reveal.

Their innocent smiles said a lot more than their words. One of them had a sparkling broad, unforgettable smile, the kind that reflects in the eyes. She watched them walk away until their balloons faded in the blue twilight, hoping, they would use their colouring books. They did say they would.

Days drifted…

One evening, she decided to find out and went to the flyover near the temple, after office hours. That's where the balloon girls lived, they had vaguely mentioned.

She spotted one of the girls who also recognized her. She asked her if she still had the colouring book. The girl lamented that her book was taken away by one of her brothers who had discoloured it black with random lines. She offered to get the girl another one, if she really wanted. Just then, their mother appeared on seeing her, an unlikely visitor under the flyover. The broad smile girl had gone for her daily balloon selling rounds, she told. She asked the mother about the children's school and studies, and as she had anticipated, it was something desired but not possible for them.

By now, it had started getting darker and it was starting to drizzle. The mother almost urged her to leave because of that. She kind of felt a slight overwhelm, moved by her genuine concern.

She was earnestly hoping to see the girl with the broad smile again, see if she filled in some colours, maybe teach her and others a few numbers and alphabets.

Many days later, she went to see them again hoping to find them under that flyover; they were like nomads on the move from one flyover to another.

It was her golden day, because, there she was, flashing her bright, broad smile. The girl hurried to get her colouring book from under the wraps of her rags. Meanwhile, she handed out the new colouring books to the other kids there.

The girl showed her the one that she loved the most amongst all the other pictures in the book; *the peacock*. She had beautifully coloured it with crayons and it looked perfect. All colours were nicely filled within the *black* lines of the peacock's sketch.

In *peach,*

green,

pink,

blue

and *purple,*

her peacock's feathers looked gorgeous.

Her eyes twinkled with the greatest luxury, that of being able to experience the joy in simple things; in her peacock colours.

She felt proud of her(self) in that moment.

Later she attempted to teach those children, simple numbers and alphabets and get them to a school.

But life happened and her attempts remain unfinished.

As we navigate through our unfinished journeys remaining open to the beautiful links between seemingly random experiences, we uncover our unique peacock colours, isn't it? Love transpires.

♥♥♥

Amazon reviews of other books by the author

"The Light at the Edges"

"Read from end to end overnight. It's brilliant, and breathtaking. The structure, maturity and theme is so vast."

"Writing is so beautiful. Used the right words for the right moments. Touched the heart."

"Reading book is like touching your soul. It connects you to your own self."

"One of the best book I have come across."

"Reading this book is an emotional journey that leaves you with a lingering sense of warmth and optimism."

"In love with writer's rhythmic writing style with expressive, comforting, and empowering power."

"With a remarkable writing style, she conveys deep thoughts in a strikingly simple manner."

"The ability to relate the poems to your real life was phenomenal."

"This book doesn't just entertain—it nurtures emotional intelligence, creativity, and quiet contemplation."

"The Cheer Collection"

"Gives you a fresh positive mindset."

"So simple & uplifting. Loved it. Gifting it as well."

"Its like one of those books to grab any time, turn any page and just feel good."

"I loved the expression clarity."

"Loved the effortless flow yet emotionally charged narrative kudos to the writer's power of expression."